Rutgers and the Water-Snouts

580 **Dana, Barbara.** Rutgers and the water-snouts. Pictures by Fred Brenner. 1969. 149p. illus. Harper, $3.95; lib. ed., $3.79. ¶ Rutgers, a lonely bulldog, becomes enamored of some curious potato-shaped prickly objects that he finds on the beach which he dubs water-snouts. Distressed by their sudden, mysterious disappearance, Rutgers enlists the aid of his companions, a mouse, a rabbit, and a badger, in searching for the water-snouts which are eventually found in the compound of porcupines who had mistakenly identified them as sick relatives. A mildly amusing story of humanized animals, similar in appeal to Gaunt's *Brim's boat* and entrancingly illustrated in black and white. Grades 3-5.

Pictures by Fred Brenner

BARBARA DANA

Rutgers
and the
Water-Snouts

HARPER & ROW, PUBLISHERS
New York, Evanston, and London

TO ALAN, ANTHONY, ADAM, MATTHEW,
MY MOTHER, MY FATHER, AND CASEY

Contents

Rutgers and the Water-Snouts

Introduction

1

Every day at four o'clock Rutgers would go down to the beach and count his water-snouts. He would stroll a purposeful sort of stroll, singing to himself as he went. The song was one he had written on the day he found his first water-snout and it went something like this:

> *Oh, a water-snout is a thing for a king,*
> *Oh, water-snout, it's of you that I sing!*
> *You can have your bananas, your coconuts too,*

You can take all your carrots, they never will do.
Take your grapes and tomatoes,
your celery and such,
*It's a water-snout that pleases me much.**
Oh, a water-snout is a thing for a king,
Oh, water-snout, it's of you that I sing!

Now you may ask how Rutgers came across these water-snouts, or who is Rutgers, or who would want a water-snout anyway if indeed there is such a thing? I shall explain.

* (He was quite proud of that line there.)

Rutgers

2

Rutgers was big for a bulldog. In fact, he was so big that his friend Marshall Rabbit had been forced to suggest that he might be a small boxer.

"I'm no small boxer," Rutgers had replied in a hurry. "I'm a bulldog is what I am. Large, maybe, but a bulldog just the same."

Rutgers was a lonely dog. He had a sad face and a heavy heart, and he would sit for hours on the beach and stare out over the ocean, trying to understand himself and exactly what it was that he was missing. Even when he was busy attending to some task that had to be attended to, there was a sadness about him, something wistful under the surface, and it was a shame.

Rutgers lived deep in the woods in a little house he had built for himself. His house was on the western coast of America, way up to the north and close to the ocean. Rutgers had taken great care in the building to be sure to keep out the ocean wind. He had used good strong boards and had nailed them firmly. The house was square with a flat roof and a sign hanging above the door. Rutgers had painted the sign himself, and it said in bold letters:

THIS IS RUTGERS' HOUSE
HELLO
YOU ANIMALS WHO PASS BY

Rutgers' house was in an area called Resnick's Territory, a beautiful territory bounded on the north by the North Woods, on the south by a fine river, on the east by mountains, and on the west by the Pacific Ocean. It had been named after Resnick, a ferret friend of Rutgers, who had taken it upon himself to deliver messages to all

animals within a certain area. The area soon became known as Resnick's Territory.

Rutgers had appointed himself watchdog for Resnick's Territory. He felt, and perhaps rightly so, that you shouldn't have a territory without a watchdog, and since he was the only dog in the area, it was clear to him the job was his.

"This job is mine," Rutgers had said to himself when he first thought about it.

One thing Rutgers was never without was his sweat shirt. It was torn in several places, but Rutgers wore it all the time. He even wore it to bed, which Marshall thought was carrying things too far. A strange thing about Rutgers' sweat shirt was that it had a large *T* written on it. Rutgers hadn't been sure he liked that when he first found the sweat shirt. He thought it should stand for something, and he couldn't think for what. Finally he decided not to worry about it.

"I'm not going to worry about this," he said. "My name will be Rutgers, and there will be this large *T* written on my sweat shirt. Who will care?"

He was right too. Everyone would ask, "What's that large *T* doing on your sweat shirt?"

Rutgers would say, "That's the *T* I found on my

sweat shirt when I found my sweat shirt," and nobody seemed to mind.

But with all this Rutgers wasn't happy, and his friends were worried.

They all agreed he was a good friend and a fine watchdog, but why wasn't he happy? Why would he sit for hours and stare out over the ocean with a sad expression?

At first they thought it might be because he was the only dog in the area, but Rutgers assured them that wasn't it.

"That's not it," Rutgers would say. "I don't mind being the only dog. It makes me feel important. It's just that something is missing."

"What's missing?" Rutgers' friends would always ask, but Rutgers didn't know.

He thought about it and thought about it, and one day he came to a decision.

"I don't know what this thing is that's missing," Rutgers said to himself, "but I'm going to look for it anyway. I'll certainly know it when I see it, and I'm not getting anywhere by sitting here and staring out over the ocean with a sad expression."

And so he began his routing. Every day he would spend hours digging in the sand, and the more he dug, the more convinced he became that he would find what he was looking for. He would pick just the perfect routing place, put his head down, and dig, throwing great piles of sand behind him. When he got down deep to where the sand was very wet, he would stick his nose down into the hole and take a good bite of sand. Then he'd pull his head up, snort several times, and move on to a new spot. When he got tired, he would sit down and stare out over the ocean.

"Someday," Rutgers would say to himself, "someday if I look hard enough, someday I'll find it."

The Discovery
of the Snouts

3

Rutgers stared at the plaque above the door
that said in very small letters:

MARSHALL
RABBIT

"Good morning to you," called Rutgers. He
knocked on the door with his right front paw. "It's
me."

"Oh, it's you," said Marshall, opening the door
and peering at Rutgers with his bright rabbit eyes.
"Come in, why don't you?"

"Just for a minute," said Rutgers, stepping into Marshall's very well-kept rabbit hole.

Everything was always in order at Marshall's house.

"You certainly keep this place up."

"I like to," said Marshall, taking a seat in his favorite oversized chair. "Neatness is nice."

"It's nice to look at," said Rutgers, "but for living in, I prefer a mess."

"Have a seat," said Marshall, ignoring Rutgers' last remark.

"Thank you just the same," said Rutgers, "but I can't stay. I was thinking you might like to join me in some routing. I'm off for the beach."

"I don't think so," said Marshall. "I'm not one for routing. I've never seen the point."

"The point," said Rutgers, "is to find what's missing."

"With all due respect," said Marshall, shifting in his chair, "I don't think anything's missing. Maybe you need a hobby. Why don't you take up some hobby like chasing things or standing on your head?"

"I have enough to do as it is," said Rutgers, turning in the direction of an unfamiliar sound.

"What is it?" said Marshall.

"An unfamiliar sound," said Rutgers. Then he turned back to Marshall. "I'm busy with my watching. I have to be ready."

"Well, you go and rout if you want to," said Marshall. "I have some cleaning to do."

"You're sure you don't want to come?" said Rutgers.

"Quite," said Marshall. "You go ahead."

So Rutgers said good-bye to Marshall and headed off in the direction of the beach. Soon he could see the water stretching out before him. It was a clear day, and the water looked very blue.

Rutgers had to climb down quite a cliff to get to the beach. He would usually slide a good part of the way, making a plunge when he got near the bottom and landing safely on the beach.

Boom! He landed and ran into the ocean, biting and growling at the waves.

"I'm here," he announced to the empty beach and then headed back to the sand to begin his routing.

He routed for more than an hour and then sat down, exhausted and discouraged.

"Maybe Marshall was right," he said to himself. "Maybe nothing's missing after all. I'll dig one more hole, and then I'll go home."

He started digging and was almost down to the very wet sand when he hit something hard.

"Hey, what's this thing that's hard?" said Rutgers, pawing at the sand with his right paw. "What is this?"

He put his nose down and put it right into something prickly.

"Ouch!" said Rutgers, backing away from the hole and shaking his head until his ears flopped hard against him. "That's prickly. Whatever that hard thing is that's down there in the sand, it's prickly."

He moved forward a few steps and peered cautiously over the side of the hole.

"I don't see it," said Rutgers very quietly to himself. "Maybe if I growl a terrifying growl, it will know I mean business and come out."

So he growled his most terrifying growl, but nothing happened.

"I'm going to dig this thing out no matter how prickly it is," said Rutgers, and he began routing furiously.

He could feel the pricklers prickling his paws, but he didn't care.

I'll show this prickler who's boss, thought Rutgers, digging harder than ever.

He dug and he dug, and suddenly up with a paw full of sand flew this hard, prickly thing which landed on the beach. Rutgers stopped digging instantly and turned around to stare at what he had routed up. He didn't move but gave it a suspicious look.

"What are you?" he said, not moving an inch, standing still as could be.

There was no answer, so Rutgers began growling a grumbling sort of growl.

Maybe it's not alive, he thought, halting his grumbling and giving the prickler a curious stare.

"This may be a perfectly harmless thing," he said to himself.

He stood there, considering, and then very slowly walked toward it and gave it a tap with his right paw.

Tap, tap! He banged it again and again, but nothing happened.

"Well," said Rutgers, "there's no harm in this. I'm going to clean the sand off it and get a better look." And he began scraping the sand away with his nails.

Then he did a very brave thing. He bent down, took the prickler in his mouth, and shook it. He shook it hard, and sand flew in all directions. The pricklers hurt his mouth a little, but it was worth it.

Suddenly he stopped, then pulled his head to one side and flung it as hard as he could, letting the prickler fall in the direction of a little pool of water among some rocks.

Splash! It landed, and Rutgers ran to the water to take a look.

It was something Rutgers had never seen before. He stared in amazement, trying to figure out what it might be. It was brownish-green in color and looked something like a potato, with little,

very little, prickly things standing out all over it.

"I've never seen anything like this," said Rutgers, trying hard to think of every brownish-green, potatolike, prickly thing he could think of.

There's never been anything like this, he thought, and then he knew.

"I've found it," said Rutgers. "I've found it; I've found what I've been looking for!"

He was so excited that he began to run around in circles, wishing there were someone he could tell.

"Water-snout!" he said in a very loud voice. "I have discovered the first allover-prickly thing that may be a vegetable that has ever been discovered, and I name it water-snout!"

He stopped suddenly and stared at the water-snout.

"I've got to find a safe place to keep you," said Rutgers. "Now that I've found you, I've got to be careful."

He waded into the pool of water, took the water-snout in his mouth, and started along the beach. Up and down he went, looking for a place to hide his water-snout.

"I think I should bury you back in the sand, water-snout," said Rutgers, "since that's where I found you. But I need a good landmark so I can always dig you up when I need you or want to show you to a friend."

Up and down the beach he searched until finally he decided on the perfect spot.

"Here we are, water-snout," said Rutgers, and he opened his mouth and let the water-snout fall to the sand right in front of a large fir tree. "This will be your house," he said, and he began digging a nice deep hole.

When he got down to where he was sure the sand was wet enough, he picked up the water-snout and dropped it into the hole.

"There you are, water-snout. I'm going to cover you up with sand now, but I'll be back to visit you very soon. Have a nice rest."

He backed away and began pushing the sand back into the hole with his nose, keeping at his job until he had the hole all filled up. Then he had to sneeze once or twice because he had gotten sand in his nose.

Rutgers stood for quite a while staring at the fir tree under which he had buried the water-snout.

"I'll certainly want to remember this tree," he said to himself. "This is the tree I'll want to remember."

He backed away from the tree, gave it a long look, and then went over and bit it near the bottom.

"There," he said. "I'll always know this tree. It's the only tree on this beach that has been bitten by me. There are my teeth marks."

He gave the tree a last look and then started off to find Marshall. On his way a little song came to him, and he sang it over and over, changing it around each time until it was just right.

Oh, a water-snout is a thing for a king,
Oh, water-snout, it's of you that I sing!

You can have your bananas, your coconuts too,
You can take all your carrots, they never will do.
Take your grapes and tomatoes,
your celery and such,
It's a water-snout that pleases me much.
Oh, a water-snout is a thing for a king,
Oh, water-snout, it's of you that I sing!

Marshall Meets
the Snouts
4

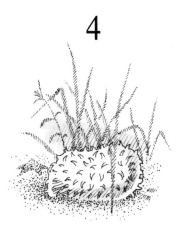

"Marshall, Marshall, open that door," said Rutgers, pounding hard on the door that led into Marshall's very well-kept rabbit hole. "It's me, and I'm here with some amazing news."

The door swung open, and out came Marshall, looking a bit sleepy. "That was an awful lot of banging," said Marshall. "What's the matter with you?"

"I've found it," said Rutgers.

"Good," said Marshall, blinking in the bright sun. "I was sleeping, taking a nap."

"This is no time for naps," said Rutgers. "I've found the very thing we've been needing."

"What's that?" said Marshall, who just remembered he had been dreaming about a fine cabbage stew.

"A water-snout!" said Rutgers.

"A what?" said Marshall.

"A water-snout!" said Rutgers. "It's been found."

"With all due respect," said Marshall, "I can't see how that's the thing we've been needing. I don't even know what a water-snout is, so how can I need it?"

"You've been needing it all the time," said Rutgers. "You just didn't know it. This is what you've been needing."

"What did I need it for?" said Marshall.

"Any number of things," said Rutgers. "Hurry up, and I'll show you."

"All right," said Marshall, "but it better not be any ordinary turnip."

"It's no ordinary turnip," said Rutgers. "You can take my word for that." And off they went to the beach.

"There," said Rutgers, uncovering the last bit

of wet sand from the top of the water-snout. "There it is!"

"Well," said Marshall, peering down at the water-snout from a safe distance.

"Give it a good look," said Rutgers. "It won't hurt you. It's a harmless vegetable."

"What's that sticking out all over it?" said Marshall.

"Pricklers," said Rutgers.

"How are we going to eat it with those pricklers sticking out all over it?" said Marshall.

"We're not going to eat it," said Rutgers. "It's not meant for eating."

"Well, what's it meant for?" said Marshall. "What good is a vegetable that's not meant for eating?"

"Plenty," said Rutgers. "There's no end to it."

"Wait a minute," said Marshall. "I'll tell you what you've got here. You've got your common prickly pear."

"Prickly what?" said Rutgers.

"Pear," said Marshall. "That's what you've got here. You've got your common prickly pear."

"What's that?" said Rutgers.

"That's what you've got here," said Marshall, waving his paw in a belittling fashion in the direction of the water-snout.

"How do you know?" said Rutgers.

"I've heard tell of them," said Marshall in a tone that suggested he'd been around. "They're small prickly desert flowers."

"This is no desert flower," said Rutgers. "It's a water vegetable is more like what it is."

"Well, what's it good for?" said Marshall.

"Time will tell," said Rutgers. "You never know with something like this."

"With all due respect," said Marshall, "I'd be very surprised if that's what we've been needing."

"You'll see," said Rutgers, and he turned to the water-snout. "I'm going to put you back in your hole now."

"Why do you talk to it like that?" said Marshall, scratching an itch behind his left ear. "There's no sense talking to a vegetable even if it is a discovery."

"That's what you do," said Rutgers. "Whenever you have a water-snout you talk to it. Good night, you water-snout." And he pushed the sand back into the hole so that only he could find it.

In the weeks that followed, Rutgers found six more water-snouts. He found them in the same

way as before, and he buried them with the first—
right at the foot of the large fir tree. He spent
hours talking to them each day, and everyone said
he was a changed dog.

"What a change in Rutgers," they would say.
"What a change since he found those water-
snouts. He's happy now. He's a happy dog."

Bad News

5

Trippler was a small white-footed mouse-friend of Rutgers, and he was always on the move. He loved to travel and could never be found in the same place twice. Whenever he and Rutgers met, it was an accident, a surprise, or a mistake of some kind, and today was no exception.

It was Thursday, and Rutgers was leaving for his daily trip to the beach. On the way, he figured out that six months ago to the day he had found his first water-snout.

There should be some kind of party today, a certain celebration, he thought to himself as he strolled along whistling his little song.

In the last six months Rutgers had grown more fond of the snouts than ever. He talked to them, cared for them, and kept them in condition for the time when they would be needed. Also he had taken to telling them his troubles. Marshall thought it was silly to tell your troubles to vegetables, but Rutgers had such a cheery outlook that Marshall let it pass.

"If it makes Rutgers happy, it must be a good thing," Marshall had reasoned.

When Rutgers arrived at the beach he headed for the large fir tree, put his head down, and began to rout as he did in just that spot each day.

They seem to be deeper than usual, these snouts, thought Rutgers as he got well down into the wet sand.

He added power to his task, getting really angry at the sand.

"Get off there, sand," he said. "I'm checking on my snouts."

Suddenly he stopped. His eyes opened wide.

"Oh, no," he whispered.

He looked at the hole and went at it again with

more force than ever, throwing great piles of sand in all directions.

"Oh, no," he said as he dug deeper and deeper.

He was down a good two feet before he stopped and admitted to himself what had happened. He sat down—motionless—all the strength gone out of him.

"They're gone," he said and started to cry.

He stayed there alone, just that way for two hours, and he might have stayed a lot longer if Trippler hadn't happened to come by.

"Rutgers, what's the matter?" said Trippler, staring at his friend.

Rutgers was crying too hard to answer, so Trippler waited a moment and then went over and took hold of Rutgers' paw.

"What's wrong?" said Trippler.

"They're gone," said Rutgers through his tears.

"What's gone?" said Trippler.

"All of them," said Rutgers. "I've been saving them and watching them and taking care of them for months, and now they're gone."

"Your snouts?" said Trippler.

"My snouts," said Rutgers.

"Are you sure?" said Trippler. "Maybe you didn't look in the right place."

"I looked in the right place all right," said Rutgers. "That's where they should be—right there in that empty hole. That's their home."

"Well, let's look for them," said Trippler. "They can't be far away."

"Oh, yes, they can," said Rutgers. "Someone must have taken them. They don't move around by themselves. They never have. I have to carry them everywhere."

"I tell you what," said Trippler. "We'll ask Marshall. Marshall always knows what to do in times like these."

"Marshall doesn't like my snouts," said Rutgers.

"He doesn't have to like them," said Trippler. "He just has to help us find them."

"It's no use," said Rutgers.

"Come on," said Trippler, pulling on Rutgers' paw. "Let's give it a try."

Trippler tugged and tugged, and at last Rutgers got up, looked sadly at the deep empty hole, and silently followed Trippler off in the direction of Marshall's house.

Marshall was at home, and when he saw the expression on Rutgers' face, he led his friends into the living room and asked them to sit down.

"Sit down," said Marshall. "What happened?"

They sat down, and Rutgers told Marshall the whole story, with Trippler filling in the places where Rutgers was too upset to go on.

"That's a shame," said Marshall, "but I'm sure we can find them. We'll think of a plan. I can speak for myself and maybe for Trippler—"

"Oh, you can speak for me," said Trippler, eager to be of whatever help he could.

"Fine," said Marshall. "I can speak for myself and for Trippler when I say that no stone will be left unturned until we find your water-snouts. We will set out on a search, and we won't give up until they're found."

"Oh, thank you," said Rutgers with the first touch of hope in his voice, "but how can we find them?"

"That," said Marshall, "will take careful planning. The first thing to do is to relax, clear our minds, and gain our strength. You sit there and do the relaxing-and-clearing-of-our-minds part, and I'll put on some soup, which will give us strength."

"It's not going to be easy, this relaxing and clearing of our minds," said Rutgers as Marshall headed for the stove.

"I know," said Marshall, "but give it a try."

A Plan
6

"I think they've been taken," said Rutgers. "That's what I think."

"Who could it have been?" said Trippler, nibbling nervously on one of his back toes.

"I don't know," said Rutgers. "Whoever took my snouts either mistook them for something else or thought they had discovered something that hadn't already been discovered by me. This someone saw my snouts and said 'Oh, here are some interesting things. I think I'll take these home and look them over.' "

"An innocent person meaning no harm," said Trippler, looking over at Rutgers to see if he had gotten the point.

"Exactly," said Rutgers.

"Now," said Marshall from over the soup, "if you don't mind my saying so, this search calls for a trip."

"A trip!" said Trippler.

"A trip," said Marshall, "that we go on and do not come back from until we've found the water-snouts."

"That's a good idea," said Rutgers.

"A trip!" said Trippler.

"This trip," said Marshall, "will mean provisions, knapsacks, and anything we might need from now on."

"Oh," said Trippler, giving a start. "I left my knapsack at Betty's."

Betty was a fat beaver who lived some distance from Rutgers and Marshall. Trippler had been visiting her last week and had left his knapsack at her dam.

"You'll get your knapsack," said Marshall, tasting the soup to see if it was hot enough. "You'll get your knapsack, but first let's make our plans."

"Betty," said Rutgers from where he was sitting in the corner.

"She's got my knapsack," said Trippler.

"Betty may have taken my snouts," said Rutgers with a far-off look in his eye.

"Why do you say that?" said Marshall. "Betty's a fine beaver."

"I know she's a fine beaver," said Rutgers, "but maybe she took them by mistake, without meaning any harm."

"Why would she do that?" said Trippler.

"I don't know," said Rutgers, "but she's a fat beaver, and I'll bet she's got them."

"What has being fat got to do with anything?" said Marshall, looking straight at Rutgers with his beady eyes and twitching nose. "Why do you say it's Betty just because she's fat? I don't see what being fat has to do with it."

"I don't either," said Trippler.

"It's not just that," said Rutgers. "Something about her makes me think she took my snouts."

"I don't see what being fat has to do with anything," repeated Marshall, somewhat for his own benefit.

"She's got all sorts of things hidden away at her

dam," said Rutgers. "The last time I was up there she served some porridge—"

"That was nice," said Marshall.

"That's not the point," said Rutgers. "She served me this porridge which was nice, and then she showed me her storage bin. All sorts of things she hoards in there. An old watch, a piece of string, a thimble, and a broken balloon."

"And my knapsack," said Trippler.

"She's not a bad beaver," said Marshall, peering into the soup with a reverent stare.

"I know," said Rutgers. "I just think if she's got all that junk, she might just be liable also to have collected my snouts."

"I'd be surprised," said Marshall. He had decided the soup was ready and began dishing it into the bowls.

"We have to start somewhere," said Rutgers, "and I say start with Betty."

"Then I could get my knapsack," said Trippler.

"All right," said Marshall as they sat down to eat their soup. "We'll start with Betty."

They all agreed and ate their soup with silent purpose.

A Visit
with Betty

7

The sun was bright, the air was cold, and the searching party was on its way. Marshall took the lead, carrying his knapsack and his map of Resnick's Territory. He had studied it carefully during the night, and he felt proud of his grasp of the existing conditions. In his mind he had outlined their search in detail with respect to geography, habitat, and available food. He looked straight ahead, clutching his map in his right paw, and led his friends on their way.

35

Rutgers followed, wearing his sweat shirt and carrying his knapsack and the extra provisions.

Trippler brought up the rear, carrying a carrot. Having left his knapsack at Betty's dam, Trippler had nothing to carry, and he complained of feeling useless and very small.

"You carry this carrot," Rutgers had said, reaching into the sack of extra provisions.

"Thank you," Trippler had replied. "I'll feel better once I get my knapsack."

"I know," Rutgers had answered.

"Sing ho for the open highway," Trippler sang out suddenly in a very loud voice. They had just crossed Rensler Brook and were heading southeast toward Betty's dam.

"What?" said Rutgers.

"Sing ho for the open road," continued Trippler, holding his head high and gripping his carrot.

"What in the world are you singing?"

"It's a little traveling song that I'm making up as we go along," said Trippler. "It's a song for the open road."

"You read that in a book," said Marshall, not bothering to turn around. "That's a very famous traveling song."

"It is not," said Trippler, quickening his pace. "I'm making it up right at this minute."

"You've heard it sung," said Marshall. "You just don't remember."

"It's nice whatever it is," said Rutgers, and he joined in the singing.

> *Sing ho for the open highway,*
> *Sing ho for the open road.*

Soon Marshall couldn't help joining in, and they all sang together.

> *Sing ho for the open highway,*
> *Sing ho for the open road.*

Betty was clumsy. There was no doubt about that, and Trippler chose to mention it as they neared her dam. They had stopped for lunch hours ago, and Marshall was already thinking about dinner.

"It's not enough to be fat," said Trippler, running a little to keep up, "but Betty has to be clumsy too."

"At least she's not mean," said Rutgers. He was still full of energy and happy to be out looking for his snouts. "Better to be clumsy than mean."

"Of course she's not mean," said Trippler. "I

know that. She's just clumsy. Good-natured and clumsy."

And that was the truth. With a proud smile on her face, Betty would bump into everything in sight. She would walk straight into trees, bushes, and shrubs and haphazardly knock over whatever was in her path.

Betty had told them it was her back feet. She had explained that they were fine for swimming, but when it came to land travel, they were only trouble and always in the way.

Marshall questioned her eyesight.

"I question her eyesight," said Marshall as they arrived within sight of Betty's dam. "Anyone who bumps into things as often as Betty does can't see anything."

"If she can't see anything," said Rutgers, "then how can she notice all those things she collects?"

"You're right," Marshall said thoughtfully. "The truth must lie elsewhere."

Just where the truth did lie they hadn't decided, but one thing was for sure. Betty was lying up ahead, headfirst in a blueberry bush.

"What's that?" said Marshall.

"That's Betty," said Rutgers. "That's the rear half of Betty sticking out from that blueberry bush."

"Betty!" said Trippler. He ran ahead and crawled in under the blueberry bush. "Can you get out?"

Betty rolled over lazily and stretched out her little front paws.

"Well, hello," said Betty. "How are you? You know you left your knapsack at my dam."

"I know," said Trippler. "I've been missing it terribly. But what happened to you? Can you get out?"

"Maybe not," said Betty in a casual tone, "but I don't mind. It's nice just lying here looking at the berries."

"You can't spend your whole life looking at berries," said Trippler, "and anyway I'm here with Rutgers and Marshall. We have to ask you a very important question."

"Well, now," said Betty, slowly pulling herself out from under the blueberry bush, "hello."

"Hello," said Rutgers. "I have to ask you this question."

"How about some porridge?" said Betty. "We

could eat some porridge while you ask me the question."

"That would be nice," said Marshall.

"It would be nice," said Rutgers, "but I can't contain myself. I have to ask you this question."

"What is it?" said Betty, twitching her small beaver ears.

"Did you happen to come across some very unusual things this week?"

"What sort of unusual things?" said Betty, leading the way to her dam. "What sort of unusual things do you mean?"

"These things," said Rutgers, "would be completely new and different. Things you never saw before."

"I don't think so," said Betty. "This wasn't much of a week. I spent most of my time hiding from a fox."

There was a hushed silence, and then Betty told her friends how the fox had almost gotten her and how she was surprised and grateful to be alive. He had come through the top of her roof, and she hadn't seen him until she happened to turn around and find him in her living room. She had escaped through her front door which led to a tunnel under

water, but it had been a close call. Another time during the week she had seen the fox giving her a piercing stare from behind a tree.

"It was a bad week," she concluded.

"It certainly was," said Rutgers. "I guess you didn't find my snouts then."

"I don't think so," said Betty. She was heading straight for a large pine tree.

"Watch out for that tree," said Marshall, but it was too late, and Betty fell over on her head.

"You've fallen over on your head," said Rutgers. "Are you all right?"

"I think so," said Betty, blinking in the bright sunlight. "It's nice down here. I like the pattern the sun makes as it shines through those leaves. Have a look, why don't you?"

"This is no time for leaves," said Rutgers. "We're talking about my snouts."

"And my knapsack," said Trippler, who was feeling smaller than ever. "You could notice me too and think of my knapsack. Consider a small mouse who has lost his knapsack."

"That's true," said Betty as Rutgers helped her to her feet. "I'm sorry. This way to my lodge."

Betty's lodge was a fine-looking hut-type dwelling made of boughs and grass and plastered with mud. Betty entered her lodge from under the water, but since her friends didn't take to water, they waited on dry land as Betty made her way into her home.

"You wait here, why don't you?" said Betty. "I'll let you in in a minute." And she walked into the stream and sank out of sight.

"She hasn't got my snouts," said Rutgers sadly as they waited by the lodge.

"That's probably true," said Marshall, making counting noises under his breath.

"What are those counting noises?" said Trippler.

"It's me," said Marshall. "I'm counting how long it takes for Betty to get inside and let us in."

"Why in the world?" said Trippler.

"Best to gather all the information you can," Marshall said absently because his mind was on the counting. "You never can tell when you'll need to know something. These matters can be important. Twenty-five, twenty-six, twenty-seven . . ."

"Come in," said Betty, poking her flat beaver head up through a hole in the top of her roof. The hole was hidden by a mass of sticks, which Betty pushed aside with her nose.

"Twenty-eight," said Marshall as he made a note on a small pad he kept stored in his knapsack.

"Come in, why don't you?" said Betty.

One by one they entered Betty's lodge through the hole in the roof and found themselves in the living room.

"How's everything in your kitchen?" said Marshall, who felt hungry.

"All right, I guess," said Betty, missing the urgency of Marshall's remark. "Sit down, why don't you?"

"I always like a nice kitchen," continued Marshall.

"What about my knapsack?" said Trippler in a very small voice. "I hope you haven't forgotten me. I'm small and it can be done."

"We haven't forgotten you," said Betty. "Your knapsack is over there in that corner."

"My knapsack, my knapsack!" cried Trippler excitedly, and he hurried over to gather it up.

"Porridge is nice on a cold day," Marshall was saying to no one in particular.

Suddenly there was a scratching sound.

"What's that?" said Rutgers.

"It's coming from the roof," said Betty.

The scratching sound continued, louder than before.

"The fox," said Betty.

"Quiet," said Rutgers sharply. "Everyone stay where you are. Don't move and don't make a sound."

"*Hic!*" said Trippler in a high hiccuping sound.

"Quiet," said Rutgers.

"*Hic!*" said Trippler.

The scratching sound got louder and louder, and soon they could see the branches that covered the hole in the roof begin to move.

"Oh, no," said Betty.

"Quiet!" said Rutgers.

"*Hic!*" said Trippler.

The branches continued to move, and a black nose could be seen pushing its way through the hole in the roof. Under the nose was a row of sharp teeth.

A New Helper

8

It was Resnick. Resnick had an important message to deliver and stuck his head right in through the hole in Betty's roof.

"A message, a message," said Resnick, pulling himself all the way into Betty's lodge. "Everyone take note of a message."

"Hic," said Trippler.

"Resnick," said Rutgers.

"Resnick," said Betty. "You scared us to death. We thought you were a fox."

"Not true," said Resnick, shaking the dry branches and twigs from his shiny coat. "Whoever told you that was misinformed. I'm a ferret."

"We know what you are," said Betty, "but we didn't think it was you. That's the thing. We thought it was someone else."

"Not true," said Resnick.

"Hic," said Trippler.

"How about joining us in some porridge?" said Marshall.

"No time," said Resnick, reaching into his mail pouch where he carried all the important messages. "Take a look at this."

He handed Marshall a yellow slip folded in half, and Marshall took it, unfolded it, and studied it with a critical gaze.

"What's up?" said Trippler, inching over to Resnick with his knapsack.

"Read the message," said Resnick. "That's the way to find out."

"Well," said Marshall, "this certainly is a situation."

"Terrible," said Resnick. "Terrible."

"What is it?" said Betty and Trippler.

Rutgers joined in. "What is it?" they all said.

"It seems," said Marshall with a slow and measured tone, "that there's a flood upstream."

"Flood upstream all right," said Resnick.

"How bad is it?" said Betty.

"Terrible," said Resnick.

"It's fairly severe," said Marshall, "but at this point it's about a mile upstream."

"Getting closer every minute," said Resnick.

"Oh, dear," said Betty, who liked the quiet, peaceful life and wasn't interested in trouble.

"Is there anything we can do?" said Rutgers.

"Not a thing," said Resnick. "Just don't go upstream. I'll keep you posted. Let you know if the danger gets worse."

"I guess that's all that can be done at this point," said Marshall. "Now let's have some of that porridge."

Betty put the porridge on, and Rutgers talked to Resnick about helping them in the search for the water-snouts. Resnick said he would be glad to help, and they worked out a plan.

Every Monday, Resnick would meet the searching party with a message containing news of the flood, plus all the information Resnick had gathered during the week that might lead to locating the water-snouts. Marshall got out his map and helped select the exact place where they would be on the following Monday. Resnick was to meet them there with the message and a food parcel that Betty would prepare. Each Monday they would decide where to meet the following week. They all agreed it was a good plan.

They spent the night with Betty and left in the early dawn when the mist was still thick and very close to the ground. Betty and Resnick waved good-bye to their friends and lost sight of them quickly.

Muskrat Burglar

9

As you know, Trippler had a strong urge to hold on to his knapsack. Being a traveling mouse, a mouse on the move, a mouse with no home but the open road, Trippler had to carry with him everything he owned in the world. This didn't amount to much.

Trippler's knapsack contained a pair of spyglasses, mouse-size, the kind for checking and keeping track of things in the distance; a watch which had belonged to Trippler's grandfather; a book of matches, standard size and too big for Trippler to light without help; and a muffler. Whenever possible Trippler would also carry a nice piece of cheese, but he didn't run into as much cheese as he would like and often had to do without.

Trippler was worried constantly that he would lose his knapsack, and he usually did. Marshall said it was because he was overanxious.

"You're overanxious about that knapsack would be my feeling," said Marshall after they had crossed the stream by Betty's lodge and begun heading north on their journey. "That's why you left it at Betty's. Whenever you're that anxious about a thing, something always goes wrong."

They traveled hard that day and made steady progress. As they went they talked about their search and how they would look. Each one had his job to do. Marshall checked everything at ground level, Rutgers checked everything below ground level by means of sniffling, and Trippler checked the bushes, trees, and shrubs, using his spyglasses.

They had lunch by a lovely pond. Trippler took his cheese out onto a water-lily pad and ate it there, basking in the bright sunlight. He could have rested there for quite some time, but Rutgers

and Marshall were eager to press on.

"Come on in off that water-lily pad," called out Rutgers when he had finished his dessert cookie. "It's time to go."

When it started to get dark, Marshall decided that it was time to bed down for the night. They certainly had made good time, and anyway Marshall was hungry. He picked out their camp-site, a rocky place up near the falls, and they sat down.

They were too tired to eat much, except for Marshall. He ate his dinner plus whatever was left over.

"Good meal," said Marshall.

Then he stretched out and fell asleep.

Trippler had just dozed off when he was awakened by the sensation that he was losing his pillow.

"I'm losing my pillow," said Trippler aloud and woke himself up. He opened his eyes and looked straight into the pointed snout of a surly muskrat. This muskrat had a firm hold on Trippler's pillow, his knapsack, and was tugging at it with glistening teeth.

"Let go, you," cried Trippler in his loudest possible voice. "Let go of my knapsack!"

The muskrat took no notice of Trippler and continued to back up, taking Trippler's knapsack with him.

"Let go!" screamed Trippler. But it was more like a squeak, and before he knew it, he felt his head bang to the ground. He could see the rear half of the muskrat as he stole into the woods, a thief in the night disappearing with everything Trippler owned in the world.

"Help me, help me!" called out Trippler. He noticed that he was wedged in between some logs in the woodpile where he had settled down for the night. "Stop, thief!"

Rutgers was the first to hear the commotion. As a watchdog, he had learned to sleep with one ear open, listening for trouble.

"Who's that?" called Rutgers. "Who's that calling for help?"

"I'm only a mouse and not big enough to defend myself," Trippler went on, almost delirious, unaware of what he was saying. "Help this mouse who's so small!"

"Trippler!" said Rutgers. "Where are you?"

"Woodpile, woodpile," said Trippler. "Help a mouse in a woodpile."

In a flash Rutgers was at the woodpile's edge.

"Are you there? Are you there?" said Rutgers.

"Here, here," said Trippler as loud as he could. "Help! Help!"

Very carefully Rutgers pushed aside the logs one by one so as not to hurt Trippler, and Trippler pulled himself free.

"Rutgers, Rutgers, he's taken my knapsack," said Trippler.

He spoke very fast, and Rutgers couldn't understand him.

"I can't understand you," said Rutgers. "What happened?"

"This muskrat made off with my knapsack," said Trippler as distinctly as he could. "I was using it for a pillow, and he stole it right from under my head."

"Which way did he go?" said Rutgers.

"That way," said Trippler, pointing off hastily to the left, "but he's far away by now."

"I'll get him," said Rutgers.

"It's no use," said Trippler.

Marshall was up by this time, and he found his friends by the woodpile.

"What's happening here?" said Marshall.

"Oh, oh," said Trippler, unable to say anything else.

"Someone made off with Trippler's knapsack,"

said Rutgers. "A muskrat, a muskrat burglar."

"Oh, dear," said Marshall. "First the snouts and now the sack."

"Everything I own in the world," said Trippler. "The whole of it."

"I know," said Marshall gravely. "I know."

"I'll get him," said Rutgers. "I'll catch that muskrat burglar."

"It would be pretty hard to get him in the dark," said Marshall. "I tell you what we'll do. We rest until dawn, and then we get him."

"I don't think I can sleep," said Trippler. "It won't be very comfortable without my pillow, and anyway I'm too upset. I'd only have nightmares."

"You sleep with me," said Rutgers. "That would be the best thing. You sleep right next to me, and then you won't be scared."

Trippler thanked Rutgers, and they settled down with Trippler curled up beside Rutgers' ear.

Trippler tended to snore. But for one thing it was a tiny mouse snore and not loud enough to disturb Rutgers, and for another thing Rutgers snored so loudly himself that he couldn't hear Trippler. Trippler put his little paws over his ears to keep out the noise of Rutgers' snoring, and they both slept soundly.

Surprise Attack
10

The dawn broke and Trippler opened his eyes.

I'm sad about something, he thought to himself, and then he remembered.

"Wake up," said Trippler as loud as he could into Rutgers' ear. "We have to find my knapsack."

"Oh, yes," said Rutgers. "That muskrat burglar."

They woke Marshall, who heated up the breakfast, and after they had eaten, they had a meeting.

"How do we capture the muskrat?" said Marshall, cleaning off his nice white coat with his rabbit tongue. "That is our question."

"I wish I'd gone after him last night," said Rutgers. "I bet I could have caught him."

"Impossible," said Trippler.

"Doubtful," said Marshall.

"That muskrat makes me mad," said Rutgers. "If it weren't for him, we could look for my snouts. Now instead we have to look for the sack."

"We better find the sack," said Trippler. "It's a very important thing. Don't forget it has the spy-glasses in it. Those will certainly be needed in looking for the water-snouts. You can be sure of that."

"I suppose so," said Rutgers, "but that muskrat still makes me mad. Interruptions, interruptions!"

"All right," said Marshall. He sat up suddenly on his hind legs and twitched his nose. "Here's what we do. Does anybody have an idea where to begin?"

Both Rutgers and Trippler said they didn't, and so Marshall continued.

"Whenever you have a problem, and you don't know where to begin," said Marshall, "this is what you do." He stopped a moment to add suspense.

"What do you do?" said Trippler.

"What you do," said Marshall, "is you examine all the information at hand."

"What information is at hand?" said Trippler. "There's no information at hand. All we know is we don't know anything."

"Wrong," said Marshall. "We know who took your knapsack."

"A muskrat," said Trippler.

"A muskrat burglar," said Rutgers.

"Right," said Marshall. "Now we make a list of everything we know about muskrats." And he went over to his knapsack and took out his pad and pencil. "Rutgers, you begin. Tell me everything you know about muskrats."

"Everything?" said Rutgers.

"Everything," said Marshall.

"It seems silly," said Rutgers.

"Tell me anyway," said Marshall.

"I feel foolish," said Rutgers.

"Never mind that," said Marshall.

"Well," said Rutgers, "they're about a foot and a half long."

"Good," said Marshall, taking notes on his pad.

"This is ridiculous," said Rutgers.

"Go on," said Marshall.

"They have a funny-looking tail," said Rutgers.

"It's long, and it doesn't have any hair on it."

"Like mine," said Trippler.

"Fine," said Marshall.

"I know something," said Trippler. "You look at a muskrat, and you think to yourself, Well there's a small beaver, when in fact he's really more of a big mouse."

"I'll accept that," said Marshall.

"Another thing I heard," said Trippler. "They love to sit on a homemade raft in the middle of a quiet pond and eat their lunch."

"Good," said Marshall.

"I never heard that," said Rutgers.

"It's true," said Trippler. "I heard it."

"That's four things," said Marshall. "Let's have one more."

"They have no distinct neck," said Trippler.

"You look at a muskrat and you say, I don't see his neck."

"Good," said Marshall.

"I don't see how this is going to help," said Rutgers.

"You will," said Marshall. "Now, briefly, here's our list."

THE MUSKRAT

1. One and a half feet long.
2. Funny-looking tail without hair on it.
3. A big mouse rather than a small beaver.

"That's not a very good one," said Trippler.

"Quiet," said Marshall.

4. They eat their lunch on a raft in the middle of a pond.
5. They have no distinct neck.

"Now what do we have?" said Rutgers impatiently. "We have a list, that's what we have. We have no muskrat, just a list of his habits."

"That's a beginning," said Marshall. "Think! Where would this muskrat burglar be at twelve o'clock today?"

"That's something we don't know," said Trippler. "If we knew that, maybe we could catch him. But that's not on the list."

"In a way it is," said Marshall. "Twelve o'clock is lunchtime, and at lunchtime he is—"

"In the middle of a pond," said Rutgers.

"Right," said Marshall.

"And there's only one pond anywhere near here," said Trippler. "I've seen Marshall's map. It's where we were yesterday."

"Right," said Marshall.

"To the pond!" said Rutgers.

"Wait!" said Marshall. "With all due respect, we can't just go to the pond. How will we capture him once we find him?"

"I know," said Rutgers. "I could make an announcement. I could stand at the edge of the pond and say, 'Attention, all those eating their lunch on this pond. Everyone who doesn't have a distinct neck, come ashore.' "

"He wouldn't come," said Trippler. "He'd suspect something."

"Trippler's right," said Marshall.

"I know," said Trippler. "Since he's really more of a big mouse, I could dress up as a big mouse, and then he'd take me for a friend."

"How could you do that?" said Rutgers. "There's no way of making you big. You're small, and that's that."

"I could eat a lot," said Trippler.

"That would take years," said Rutgers.

"Wouldn't work," said Marshall, staring hard at their list of muskrat habits.

"Then here's another thing," said Trippler. "How about this? A muskrat is really more of a big mouse, and what would a mouse be scared of?"

"A giant cat," said Rutgers.

"That's it," said Trippler.

"But where do we find this giant cat?" said Rutgers. "We don't even know any giant cats."

"Marshall could disguise himself," said Trippler. "Marshall could disguise himself as a giant cat."

"I could not," said Marshall. "I don't have a giant-cat costume. He'd know."

"Surprise attack," said Rutgers. "It's the only way."

"That sounds good," said Marshall. "Keep talking."

"Well," said Rutgers, "in order to surprise him we must get to the pond before he does."

"Before lunchtime," said Trippler.

"Before lunchtime," said Rutgers. "We get to the pond at eleven o'clock. That's the first part of the surprise. The second part of the surprise is that Marshall goes to one side of the pond, Trippler to another, and I go to a third."

"That's three surprises," said Trippler.

"All right," said Rutgers, "three surprises."

"Four all together," said Trippler. "There's also the getting-to-the-pond-before-he-does part."

"All right," said Rutgers. "Four surprises. Now we wait, each on different sides of the pond. At twelve o'clock we see the muskrat. He boards his raft."

"With my knapsack," said Trippler.

"Right," said Rutgers. "He boards the raft with Trippler's knapsack and heads for the middle of the pond to eat his lunch. As he starts to eat, Trippler starts talking."

"Why do I do that?" said Trippler.

"You're a decoy," said Rutgers.

"Why me?" said Trippler.

"Let me finish," said Rutgers. "You're a decoy, and you say 'Come back here with my knapsack, you muskrat burglar.'"

"He won't come," said Trippler.

"Right," said Rutgers. "He knows you'll be after him to get your knapsack back, and he knows Marshall and I will be helping you because he saw us at the campfire together. He also knows that Marshall and I are stronger than you."

"Because you're so much bigger," said Trippler.

"Because we're so much bigger," said Rutgers. "And he'll say to himself 'This small mouse is a decoy,' and he'll be right. And he'll look in the other direction for the real attacker. He will look in the other direction for the real attacker, and there will be Marshall holding a big stick."

"But that's no surprise," said Trippler. "He looked for Marshall, and there he was."

"He looked for Marshall, and there he was," said Rutgers. "But the surprise will be that Marshall is also a decoy. The real attacker will already have swum up behind the raft, have taken the knapsack in his teeth, and be on his way back to shore. That attacker will be me."

"Oh, my," said Trippler, who was very impressed with Rutgers' plan.

"Good plan," said Marshall, who was impressed also. "Good plan!"

Capture

11

They headed back in the direction of the pond, moving very quietly in case the muskrat should be on his way to the pond too.

Even though they were early, they were taking no chances.

They arrived at the pond at eleven o'clock as scheduled, and the muskrat was nowhere in sight. Just then Trippler got another case of the hiccups.

"Hic!" said Trippler.

"Quiet," said Rutgers. "Why do you do that?"

"I can't help it, *hic,*" said Trippler.

"Well, it's a good thing you're the decoy," said Rutgers. "That's all I can say. It's all right for a decoy to have the hiccups. He's supposed to attract attention."

"Hic," said Trippler.

"If you were the attacker," said Rutgers, "we'd really be in trouble."

"That's true," said Marshall.

"Hic," said Trippler.

"Now, Trippler," said Rutgers, "you take your hiccups and go around to the eastern side of the pond. As soon as you see the muskrat in position in the middle of the pond, make all the noise you can."

"OK," said Trippler. *"Hic!"* And he was off.

Marshall found a large stick and headed around for the western side of the pond, ready to pretend to be the attacker but really to be another decoy. Rutgers waited where he was, keeping down very low in the underbrush so as not to be seen. Then they waited.

At exactly twelve o'clock the muskrat appeared at the far side of the pond. Rutgers watched him as he boarded a small homemade raft and headed out for the middle of the pond. Just as they suspected, he had Trippler's knapsack.

Trippler could be heard hiccuping loudly from the eastern side of the pond. When the muskrat got out near the center of the pond, he seemed to turn in Trippler's direction. As the muskrat bit into a choice piece of cheese Trippler started calling. "Come back here, *hic*, with my knapsack you, *hic*, muskrat burglar, *hic*," called Trippler as loud as he could.

Rutgers could see the muskrat peering in Trippler's direction and heard him call, "You can't fool me, you mouse. You've got me surrounded."

Then Rutgers saw the muskrat turn around and Marshall pop out from behind a bush with his large stick.

"Aha!" said Marshall in a menacing tone, holding his large stick over his head.

"I knew it," said the muskrat. "There's my attacker!"

Rutgers dove into the water and swam as fast as he could toward the muskrat's homemade raft. The muskrat had dropped his cheese and was up on his hind legs, shouting abusive things at Marshall.

"Come and get me, you rabbit," said the

muskrat. "You think you're so tough! Let's see you swim."

"Aha!" said Marshall as fiercely as he could, not moving an inch.

"Come on," said the muskrat. "Scared of a little water?"

Rutgers had reached the back of the raft. He very carefully raised his head and took Trippler's knapsack between his teeth.

"Aha!" said Marshall.

"Come and get me," said the muskrat.

Rutgers slowly lifted the knapsack up off the raft and turned to swim back to shore. He held the knapsack very high to be sure it didn't get wet.

But it was hard to swim that way, and Rutgers couldn't help making splashing noises.

Marshall noticed this and tried to talk as loudly as possible.

"Aha, muskrat! Aha!" said Marshall.

Trippler hiccuped louder than ever.

The muskrat continued to shout at Marshall. "I'm coming after you," he shouted. "Nobody holding a big stick yells at me and gets away with it."

Splash! Rutgers made a terribly loud splashing sound, and the muskrat turned around.

"Who's there?" shouted the muskrat, and then he saw Rutgers. "Stop, thief!" shouted the muskrat,

and he plunged into the water after Rutgers.

It was very hard for Rutgers to swim. But he tried as hard as he had ever tried anything in his life, and he beat the muskrat to the shore!

Trippler and Marshall had both run as fast as possible to join Rutgers at the water's edge. As the muskrat started out of the water they stood in line and shouted things like *"You're* the thief!" "Go away, muskrat burglar!" and "My cousin is a giant cat!"

Marshall still had his stick, and the muskrat had no weapon at all.

I have no weapon at all. I'm outnumbered, and their cousin is a giant cat! thought the muskrat to himself, and he turned around and dove into the water and swam with all the speed he could back to his raft.

"Hooray for Rutgers!" said Trippler. "Thank you, thank you."

Rutgers loosened his grip on Trippler's knapsack, and Trippler took it in both paws, sat down, and peered inside to see if anything was missing.

"Not a thing missing!" said Trippler. "Everything I own in the world safe at last!"

"Good work, Rutgers," said Marshall, setting down his large stick.

"Thank you," said Rutgers. He was exhausted and panted hard.

"Now the snouts," said Marshall. "Next we find the water-snouts!"

Badger Meeting
12

Marshall had his map out and was giving it his full attention. "East is east, and west is west," he was saying, "and where we are is the question."

"That's the question all right," said Trippler from where he sat, hunched over and shivering near a bush. He had his muffler wound around his neck three times for extra warmth. "It's all well and good to talk about your directions, to theorize. But until we know where we are, we're lost

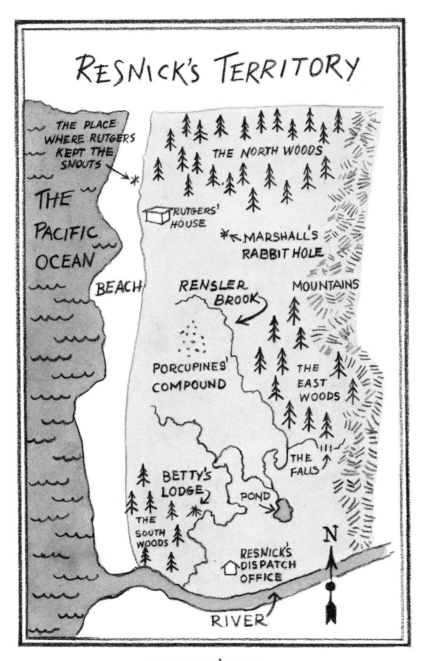

MARSHALL'S MAP

and that's that. It's freezing too, in case you hadn't noticed."

"In due time," said Marshall, peering at the crumpled paper in search of a landmark, "in due time things will be arranged."

After their episode with the muskrat, they had reorganized their search. Marshall felt that they needed to be more specific in their looking and had presented an outline of how they should proceed. When Trippler had heard about it, he had objected. "Why do we need to be more specific?" Trippler had inquired. "We each have our job to do. You can't get more specific than that."

"Not good enough," Marshall had replied.

Then he had presented the outline. It went like this:

SEARCH FOR SNOUTS

1. Follow up all clues.
2. Cover Resnick's Territory:
    a. Ask every animal we notice.
    b. Keep eyes open.
3. Meet Resnick weekly.

Trippler had complained about Point 2b, arguing that he always kept his eyes open unless he was asleep. And when he was asleep, he wasn't looking for snouts.

"That's common outline usage," Marshall had explained. "It's understood."

"Not by me," Trippler had replied.

Aside from Trippler's feelings about Point 2b, both he and Rutgers were impressed with the outline.

"That's a good outline," they had said. But so far the search has been unsuccessful.

They had been searching for over a week, and there was still no sign of the missing water-snouts. Monday had passed and with it their meeting with Resnick. Resnick had brought food and many messages, but not one of them had anything to do with the water-snouts. They heard news of the flood which was nearing Betty's dam, of bad weather in the north, and of a shortage of nuts in the East Woods, but no news of the snouts.

Rutgers was a very unhappy dog indeed. "My snouts, my snouts," he would sometimes mutter in a sad and wistful tone, but otherwise he said very little.

As Marshall studied his map Rutgers stared at the ground. He didn't notice the cold wind that whistled through the trees and made Trippler's nose feel like someone was giving it a hard pinch.

"There we have our east," said Marshall, pointing off to the right, "and here we have our west."

"Nothing is as cold as a cold mouse," said Trippler suddenly in a kind of proclamation. But nobody paid any attention.

"Now," said Marshall, setting down his map and looking at his friends with his pink rabbit eyes. "We have a situation here."

"That's the truth," said Trippler. His nose had turned blue.

"We have a situation here," continued Marshall, "and the situation is this. We are in a certain place, but we don't know where that certain place is. Once we know where the certain place is, then we will know where we are. And once we know where we are, we can determine in which direction to go to get to another place."

"That makes sense," said Trippler.

"Now," said Marshall, "how do we find out where we are?"

They discussed their problem and came up with an idea. They would start walking, and as they walked they would look as hard as they could for something familiar. They gathered their things and set out with Marshall leading the way, Trippler following behind him, and Rutgers sadly bringing up the rear.

They covered much ground, but nothing looked familiar. Trippler had his spyglasses out and was examining everything at close range. Suddenly he cried out, "Stop."

"Something familiar?" said Rutgers.

"Over there on that knoll," said Trippler.

"Over there on that knoll what?" said Rutgers.

"Over there on that knoll I see a traveler," said Trippler.

Rutgers took the spyglasses from Trippler and peered through one of the tiny mouse-size lenses. He couldn't use them both at once because one lens fell just at the bridge of his nose.

"Oh," said Rutgers, "that's a strange-looking traveler."

"Let me see," said Marshall, taking the glasses from Rutgers. "Badger," said Marshall. "That's a traveling badger."

"Point 2a," said Rutgers, remembering Marshall's outline. "Ask everyone we notice."

"Never mind about 2a," said Trippler. "Let's find out where we are."

The badger was looking in another direction

and didn't see the small group approaching from behind.

"Hello, badger," said Trippler. "Got a question for you."

"Who's there?" said the badger, slowly turning his great flat head in Trippler's direction. His tiny badger ears stuck out on either side of his head and appeared to have been put there by mistake. More careful planning would have placed them further up on his crown.

"We're lost," said Trippler, "and we must find our way. Do you know where we are?"

The badger sat down and thought for a minute.

"Oh, yes," he said.

"Could you tell us?" said Trippler.

"You're at the northeastern tip of the East Woods," said the badger. "In fact that's where we all are. I'm here too as you can see."

"Oh, thank you, badger," they all said.

"Don't mention it," said the badger, still sitting down.

"Have you seen or heard tell of anything strange lately?" said Rutgers, asking the question he had repeated so many times since the search had begun.

"What sort of thing?" said the badger.

"Any sort of thing," said Rutgers. "Anything at all."

"No," said the badger thoughtfully. "Nothing strange."

"Oh," said Rutgers.

"I see by your knapsack that you are a traveler," said Trippler. "Where are you bound for?"

"Nowhere much," said the badger.

"Just out for a good time?" said Trippler.

"Not really," said the badger.

"What are you out for?" said Trippler.

"Well," said the badger, and then he paused for a long time, his thoughts seeming to wander.

"Weather's not much good for traveling," said Trippler.

"It's my birthday," said the badger.

"Happy birthday," they all said. "Happy birthday, badger."

"Thank you," said the badger.

"But why are you traveling?" said Trippler.

"I figured I should do something," said the badger.

"Didn't anybody give you a party?" said Rutgers.

"No," said the badger. "If they did, they didn't tell me about it."

They all felt sorry for the lonesome badger. They explained that although they didn't have time to give him a party he was welcome to join them in their search. The badger said he would like that and told them that he might even turn out to be useful. "I may not be much to look at, but I'm great at digging," he explained. "I can easily outdistance a man with a shovel."

They all agreed that the badger might turn out to be very useful indeed and also pointed out that he was a fine-looking badger.

"It's not everyone who has a white stripe down the middle of his face," said Trippler, and the badger had to agree.

"What's your name?" said Rutgers as they readied themselves to move on.

"I don't have one," said the badger.

"No name?" said Rutgers. "Didn't anyone ever give you a name?"

"If they did, they didn't tell me about it," said the badger.

"We could give you one," suggested Trippler.

"No, thank you," said the badger. "If I were supposed to have a name, I would have had one long before this. I'll do without."

"Whatever you say," said Rutgers.

They decided to head for Resnick's Dispatch Office, their meeting place for that week. They traveled hard, and as they moved south the weather began to warm up. Trippler took off his muffler and put it back into his knapsack. They crossed through the entire East Woods before nightfall, making very good time. The presence of their new friend made them feel more hopeful, as if a new chapter were beginning. At one point Rutgers even broke into song.

> *My friends and I will find my snouts,*
> *We'll find my snouts in the morning.*
> *I'll take them home and keep them safe*
> *And they won't mind my snoring.*

Trippler felt strongly that snoring should be changed to something that rhymed better with morning, but he was so glad to see Rutgers happy that he kept his thoughts to himself.

Rutgers Gets
a Sore Throat

13

Rutgers had a sore throat. He had tried every-thing—hot tea, lemonade, salt water, and extra rest—but nothing seemed to help. He talked less than ever, and when he did it was only a froglike croak that scared Trippler.

"Oh, help!" Trippler would cry out whenever Rutgers tried to speak.

"It's only Rutgers," Marshall would explain.

The badger was the only happy one. He already

felt at home with his new friends and was glad to be out looking for something, even if he wasn't quite sure what it was that he was looking for.

It was Monday and the weary group was slowly making its way toward Resnick's Dispatch Office. Each of them hoped—but without much conviction—that Resnick would have an answer, a clue, an idea of some kind that would save the day. They were all tired, especially Trippler. He took deep breaths for extra oxygen and had to sit down every so often because of pains in his tiny mouse legs.

Resnick's Dispatch Office was really more of a shack. There were holes in the roof and cracks in the walls, and the sign outside had faded from being out in the weather. Many of the letters had been washed away by the rain, and Resnick hadn't bothered to repair them. The sign presently read

NICK'S
PATCH
OFF

and it confused everybody.

"Nick's Patch Off," said Marshall, fixing his beady eyes on the weather-worn sign. "That's not altogether clear."

"It's not a bit clear," said Trippler, puffing to

get his breath. They had just climbed a steep hill.

"According to the map, this should be Resnick's Dispatch Office," said Marshall, "not Nick's Patch Off."

"Nick's Patch Off," said Trippler aloud, trying to get the sense of it.

"Never heard of it," said the badger.

"What can it mean?" croaked Rutgers.

"Oh, help!" cried Trippler.

"It's only Rutgers," Marshall explained.

They all sat down in front of the strange sign and thought about it.

"Whatever a Patch Off is," said Trippler, "it belongs to Nick."

"You're probably right," said Marshall, "but with all due respect, this Nick should have explained things better. A Patch Off is not a common term."

"Never heard of it," said the badger.

"Patch Off," repeated Trippler several times. "Maybe it's a place for taking off patches."

"Patches of what?" said the badger, his ears bending downward in confusion.

"Different kinds of patches," said Trippler. "I have a patch on my knapsack for instance."

"I don't think so," said Marshall. "With all due respect, a patch is to be put on. You don't put a patch on until there's a hole in something, and once there's a hole in something, it needs a patch on, not a patch off."

"That's true," croaked Rutgers.

"Oh, help!" cried Trippler.

"Hello," said a voice from inside the shack. "What are you doing sitting out there in front of my sign?"

"It's Nick," said Trippler, jumping to his feet. "He may be armed."

"Not necessarily," said Marshall.

The door of the shack swung open, and there stood Resnick with a green visor on his forehead and two armbands around his upper forearms.

"Resnick," cried Trippler, "what are you doing here?"

"What am I doing here?" said Resnick. "It's my office."

"No, it's not," said Trippler. "It's Nick's Patch Off. The sign says so."

"Not true," said Resnick. "Come in."

Trippler kept pestering Resnick until finally Resnick explained what had happened to the sign.

"The rain washed off some of the letters," said Resnick, taking a seat behind his large desk. "No time to fix it."

"That explains it," said the badger.

"Who's he?" said Resnick, noticing the badger for the first time.

"Our new friend," said Marshall. "We were lost, and he helped us find our way."

"Oh," said Resnick.

The office was a mess. Piles of papers, pamphlets, maps, pencils, and guide books lay everywhere, and a naked light bulb hung above the desk. The office had at one time belonged to a forest ranger, and when Resnick took it over, he became the only animal in the territory to be blessed with electricity.

"It's good I've got this electricity," Resnick had reasoned. "I may need to write down a message at any time of the day or night."

"Any news?" croaked Rutgers.

"Oh, help!" cried Trippler.

"You'd better be quiet, Rutgers," said Marshall. "You keep scaring Trippler. I'll find out all there is to know about the snouts."

"Well," said Resnick, looking out from under his green visor. "No definite news, but I do have some clues."

"Clues!" croaked Rutgers.

"Oh, help!" cried Trippler.

"One," said Resnick, "an unidentified vegetable was sighted Thursday night on the southern bank of the river, opposite the South Woods. A mole requested information about it, but none was available."

"That might be a snout," croaked Rutgers.

"Oh, help!" cried Trippler.

"Two," said Resnick, "a groundhog three miles to the north reported an unusual potato. Wanted all potatoes in the area checked. They haven't been as yet."

Rutgers had a strong feeling about the river. After all, the snouts were water-snouts and would most likely be near the water.

They thanked Resnick several times, and Resnick gave them their food parcel.

"It's a little smaller than usual," said Resnick, handing over the parcel. "Betty's been very worried about the flood, and she's been spending most of her time upstream helping with the dams."

"Don't tell me," said Marshall, staring at the tiny parcel in dismay. "This won't last the week."

"Try to make it last," said Resnick. "That's all there is."

They waved good-bye to Resnick and set out for the river.

Downriver
14

When they got to the river it was almost night. They decided to camp for the night near the water's edge and head downriver in the morning. The sky looked threatening, and they figured if a storm were coming up, they had better stay put for the night.

Marshall carefully rationed out the food. He divided what there was first into four portions— one very tiny one because a mouse eats very little— and then divided each portion into seven sections, each of the seven sections into three parts, one for each meal of the day.

When he handed out the portions for that evening everyone complained.

"Do you think I like it?" said Marshall. "I don't like it one bit, but that's all there is."

When they were ready for bed, the badger set down his knapsack and stood on his head.

"What are you doing?" said Trippler, finishing up his evening cheese.

"Going to sleep," said the badger.

"On your head?" said Trippler.

"No," said the badger. Then he fell over on his side.

"Why were you standing on your head?" said Trippler.

"It's my way," said the badger.

"Your way of what?" said Rutgers, giving the badger a curious look.

"My way of lying down," said the badger.

Just then the rain began, and they huddled together in the hollow of a fallen spruce. Trippler crawled inside the sleeve of Rutgers' sweat shirt, first begging Rutgers not to make any sudden noises. The badger curled up at Rutgers' back, and Marshall curled up next to the badger. The

tree partly shielded them from the rain, but soon the thunder and lightning began. Trippler crawled further up into Rutgers' sleeve, and the other three covered their ears with their paws. They were a lonely, wet, and frightened group that night, and none of them got much sleep.

The morning was beautiful. Bright sunlight poured through the branches of the trees, and the birds sang loudly.

Rutgers went down to the riverbank and looked out across the river, wondering if his snouts were out there somewhere. He sat alone for several minutes. Then he went back to wake up the badger.

"Could you come with me?" said Rutgers. "I have something to tell you."

The badger followed Rutgers to the river's edge, and there they sat, Rutgers describing in detail his precious snouts and the badger listening with his ears perked up in interest.

For Rutgers, talking about his snouts was the next best thing to being with them, and for a brief time he was happy.

"Well," said Trippler, bounding up behind the badger. "You'll never guess what I found."

"What?" said the badger, turning and peering down at the tiny mouse.

"A raft, that's what," said Trippler.

"A raft," said Rutgers. "That could carry us downriver."

"I know," said Trippler. "And then there is the getting to the other side. That's where the vegetable was sighted, you know."

"I know," said Rutgers.

They went back to get Marshall and found him staring sadly into a rusted tin bowl.

"What are you doing staring into that bowl?" said Trippler.

"That's where my breakfast was," said Marshall in a plaintive tone.

"Where is it now?" said Rutgers.

"I ate it," said Marshall.

"And you're still hungry?" said Rutgers.

"Very," said Marshall.

"Think about lunch," said Rutgers. "And listen, Trippler has found a raft, a raft that will take us downstream."

They packed up and followed Trippler in the direction of the raft.

"There it is," said Trippler, bounding up ahead of the others.

It was an old raft, and it had several holes in it, but they figured it was strong enough to get them where they were going.

"We'll take it," said Marshall after studying the raft for several minutes.

"Here's something," said the badger. He had come across a paddle and was dragging it in the direction of the raft.

"That's fine," said Marshall. "We'll need that paddle."

They climbed aboard, and the badger pushed at the riverbank with the paddle to set the raft free and drive it out toward the center of the river. He had agreed to do the steering and started them off downriver at a steady pace.

Their trip was fairly smooth until they got about a mile from the mouth of the river. Marshall had just handed out the lunch when a great surge of water carried them sideways and spun the raft halfway around in a circle.

"Help, help!" cried Trippler, clutching his knapsack in one paw and his cheese in the other.

Marshall pointed downriver and said they should be going that way.

"We know," said Rutgers. "Strong current!"

"That way," directed Marshall, trying to keep busy and not worry about drowning.

The badger almost had the raft back on course when there was another sudden rush of current and they spun around in a complete circle. Trippler reached out desperately for something to hold onto and dropped his knapsack into the river.

The Sack Hunt
15

"It's in the river," said Trippler, anxiously peering over the side of the raft.

"I'm afraid so," said Marshall. He was holding very tightly to Trippler's tail lest Trippler fall into the water.

"You can have mine," said the badger, working steadily with the paddle.

"You don't understand," said Trippler. "My knapsack is special. Everything I own is in that sack. I have no home you see, no home but the open road. I carry everything with me."

"Oh," said the badger.

"It's a nightmare," said Rutgers.

"My knapsack, my knapsack," said Trippler.

"We'll get it back," said Marshall. "Don't worry."

With some difficulty the badger brought the raft over to the southern riverbank, and the animals climbed onto dry land.

"A sack hunt," said Rutgers as they gathered in a little group by the water's edge. "This is no snout hunt. It's a sack hunt."

"Whatever it is," said Marshall, "we have a problem."

"You're not kidding," said Trippler.

"Our problem is this," said Marshall. "Trippler's knapsack has fallen into the river and must be gotten back."

"Right," said the badger.

"It's a nightmare," said Rutgers.

"Now," said Marshall, "who among us is a good enough swimmer to get it back?"

"I don't swim," said the badger suddenly, forlornly, a devastating pronouncement.

"None of us do," said Marshall, "none of us

except Rutgers, and even Rutgers is no underwater swimmer."

There was a long silence while each of them pondered what in the world could be done. Each wished with all his heart that he could be the one to say "I can do it!" "I'll go down!" —but each of them knew the job would be too much for him.

Suddenly Rutgers raised his head. His ears went forward and his eyes opened wide and clear.

"Betty!" he said, his voice full of excitement. "Betty can do it!"

"That's right," they all cried. "Betty! Of course!"

"Now here's what we do," said Rutgers. "The three of you wait here marking the place where the knapsack was dropped while I swim back across the river and get Betty. I'll be as fast as I can. Don't anybody move."

"Good plan," said Marshall, and the others agreed.

Rutgers left quickly, plunging into the water and crossing the river with ease.

As they waited by the river the badger led them in song.

"Here's a song I learned in the badger brigade,"

said the badger, sitting up on his hind legs. "It goes like this."

When you're blue
And you don't know what to do,
Sing a song.
If you mope
And you haven't got a hope,
Sing a song.
Courage, badgers,
Courage, all,
Hold your heads up
Proud and tall.
When you're scared
And you feel you're unprepared,
Sing a song!

When he got to the "Courage, badgers" part, the badger interrupted himself and said that they could change that line around to suit themselves.

Marshall and Trippler thought about it, but nothing else seemed to fit. Trippler suggested changing it to "Courage all you animals waiting for Rutgers and Betty to come back," but Marshall pointed out that it destroyed the rhythm.

"It's too long, and it destroys the rhythm," said Marshall.

Finally they decided to change it to "Courage, animals" which, as Marshall pointed out, was still too long but would have to do.

The tune was simple, and they caught on quickly, singing it many times.

When you're blue
And you don't know what to do,
Sing a song.
If you mope
And you haven't got a hope,
Sing a song.
Courage, animals,
Courage, all,
Hold your heads up
Proud and tall.
When you're scared
And you feel you're unprepared,
Sing a song!

Beaver Rescue
16

Rutgers sped through the South Woods, taking no time to rest. When he got to Betty's lodge, there was Betty tugging on a large branch.

"Betty, we need you!" cried Rutgers.

"Well, Rutgers," said Betty, dropping the branch and tumbling backward into a peculiar half-sitting position. Her hind legs stuck out in front of her, slightly in the air.

"Come quickly," said Rutgers. "You're needed at the river."

"At the river?" said Betty.

"Yes," said Rutgers. "Trippler lost his knapsack, and we need you to get it back."

"Well, sure," said Betty, and she fell over on her back, her feet straight up in the air. "Is there time for porridge?"

"No time for porridge," said Rutgers. "We have to hurry!"

"I'm sorry about your food parcel," said Betty, slowly bringing herself to her feet. "I've been worried about the flood. It's getting very close, you know."

"We heard," said Rutgers. "That's a shame."

Betty took an extra moment and went down into her storage bin. When she came up again, she had a large brown package in her mouth.

"Bread," she said. "You must all be starving."

Betty had great difficulty understanding the urgency of the situation. Perhaps she would understand for a moment, but then something would catch her attention, and she'd forget all about it. As they headed for the South Woods Rutgers called out to her for the fifth time.

"Come on, Betty," he shouted.

Betty had noticed an interesting beetle and was

watching its progress as it moved across a large flat rock.

"This is no time for beetles," said Rutgers.

Rutgers now carried the bread. Betty had tried to take it at first, but the extra weight ruined whatever balance she had and caused her to fall over on her nose. Rutgers had quickly taken the package from Betty.

"Let me carry that," Rutgers had said. "We'll never get there if you keep falling over on your nose like that."

Betty bumped into several trees on the way, making the trip back to the river quite long. When at last they reached the riverbank, it was almost dusk.

"There they are!" shouted Trippler when he saw Rutgers and Betty appear from out of the woods on the far side of the river.

Betty sank into the river and swam in her effortless beaver way to greet her friends on the other side. Rutgers followed close behind her, still carrying the bread.

"What's in that brown package?" said Marshall, eyeing the bundle with a greedy stare. "Is it food by any chance?"

"Bread," said Betty.

"That's a wonderful thing," said Marshall in a reverent tone, and he picked up the package and put it away with the other food.

They introduced the badger to Betty which as it turned out was unnecessary since they had met at a campfire meeting two years back. Then they set to work.

It was getting darker by the minute, and Betty was urged to make haste.

"Please hurry," said Trippler. "Night will fall, and my sack will be lost forever—everything I own in the world."

Betty walked into the river and sank quickly out of sight. The others sat in a line along the water's edge, waiting and hoping.

Seven times Betty traveled to the bottom of the river, scouting its every inch for the missing knapsack. Each time she reappeared on the surface of the water Trippler became more despondent. Soon he took to a quiet kind of sobbing, and no one could comfort him.

"That's the end," he said through his tears. "Why torture myself?"

When it came time for Betty to make her eighth trip down, Trippler wouldn't even watch.

Betty disappeared out of sight, and they waited.

She stayed down for such a long time that they began to worry. The minutes passed, and at last Rutgers decided to go down after her.

"You can't do that," said Marshall. "You're no underwater swimmer. You'd only drown."

"I must," said Rutgers. "I can't stand it."

Just then Betty's brown beaver head appeared on the surface of the water. Trippler's knapsack was gripped firmly between her teeth.

"Your knapsack, your knapsack!" they all cried, and Trippler turned around.

He said nothing but held out his paws as Betty brought the knapsack up out of the water.

"Here you are," said Betty, smiling a big smile.

Large tears poured down Trippler's cheeks, but they were tears of joy.

Mole Meeting

17

The badger woke up at six o'clock with a compulsion to go after the mole. Resnick's words rang loudly in his head as he opened his eyes and peered into the early morning fog. "An unidentified vegetable was sighted on the southern bank of the river. A mole requested information about it," Resnick had said.

The badger could hear the words as clearly as if Resnick were standing right there, and he knew what had to be done.

"Get thee to the mole," cried a voice from within, and the badger sat up on his hind legs.

"I've got to get to that mole," he said.

All other thoughts had left the badger's mind. He could think only of the mole, only that he must find him—whoever he might be, wherever he might be—find him and thereby solve the mystery of the missing water-snouts.

The badger stood up, pointed his nose to the west, and followed it in the direction of the sea.

It was after nine when Rutgers woke up. The other animals were still asleep. Betty had stayed the night and was stretched out near a mound of earth, snoozing and smiling broadly. Rutgers couldn't help thinking what a fine beaver friend he had in Betty. Such a fine friend to leave her home in a time of danger and go off after a sunken knapsack.

Clumsy she is, thought Rutgers to himself, but she's among the best.

Trippler was still somewhat in shock. He had all four paws wound tightly around his knapsack and slept in a determined clench. He looked very uncomfortable. Every muscle was tense. His head rested on a rock, and he wore an anxious expression. Rutgers was amazed that he could get any sleep that way.

Marshall slept by the side of the provisions in a businesslike way. Shortly he sat up and said it was time for breakfast.

"I wonder where the badger went," said Rutgers as Marshall opened the package of bread that Betty had brought the night before.

"Where could he be?"

"He'll miss his breakfast if he doesn't show," said Marshall, dividing up the food.

All through breakfast Trippler wouldn't put down his knapsack. He ate with one paw, the other tightly clutching the sack, and he made a terrible mess. Large crumbs of bread fell all around him.

"Look at that terrible mess you're making," said Marshall, giving Trippler a scornful stare. "That's wasteful I'm sure you realize."

"Can't help it," said Trippler. "I'm not putting this sack down for anything."

When they finished eating, Betty said she had to go. They thanked her several times for retrieving Trippler's knapsack, and she said it was her pleasure.

Trippler was so appreciative that he considered giving her the watch that had belonged to his grandfather. He had been thinking about it all morning, but when it finally came time for Betty to go, he couldn't do it. After all, the watch had belonged to his grandfather, and it just seemed to him that he should always keep it with him. He gave Betty his biggest mouse-size kiss, which wasn't very big, and watched her swim back across the river and disappear into the woods.

"Oh, dear, where can the badger be?" said Trippler as he and Rutgers and Marshall sat by the river's edge. It was nearly lunchtime, and there was still no sign of their flat-headed friend.

"You heard that in a song," said Marshall,

turning to peer at the mouse from over his left shoulder.

"I did not," said Trippler. "I'm just asking a question."

"It's not like him to go off like this," said Rutgers.

"With all due respect," said Marshall, "he might have let us know where he was going. He might have known we would worry."

"And worse than that," said Rutgers, "we should be out looking for the snouts. And what do we do? We wait. We don't look; we just wait. This whole search has been one big interruption."

They decided to wait one more hour, and if the badger didn't come by that time, they would go on without him. Maybe he was tired of their company, they reasoned, and was afraid to tell them so.

They sat in a row on the riverbank, Marshall looking in all directions, Trippler clutching his knapsack, and Rutgers—a very sad dog indeed—staring into the distance.

Meanwhile the badger had found the mole. He had followed his nose straight to the west, and there—just at the point where the river meets the sea—there on the southern riverbank he found

him. The badger first caught sight of his pointed nose sticking out from the damp black earth, and he gathered that the mole was coming up from some kind of underground excavation.

"There he is!" said the badger. "I've got to talk to that mole!"

He doubled his speed and soon came face to face with the soft furry rodent.

"Stop, mole!" called out the badger in his strongest possible voice.

"Who goes there?" said the mole suspiciously, looking straight at the badger.

The mole was now completely up from underground, and dirt still clung to his soft, black coat.

"A friend," said the badger. "I mean no harm. I'm looking for a certain strange vegetable, and I hear that you've got one."

"I've got one all right," said the mole, nodding his head gravely. His eyes were so small that the badger thought maybe he didn't have any.

"Did Resnick send you?" said the mole.

"That's right," said the badger.

"I got a message from him this morning," said the mole. He shook himself furiously to get the dirt out of his coat. "Thought there would be more of you."

"There's only me," said the badger. "Now can I see the vegetable?"

"This way," said the mole.

The badger followed the mole several yards to the left where the mole stopped, bent forward, and began digging.

"I keep it buried," said the mole, attacking the earth with his strong forelimbs. "Can't take any chances."

The badger's heart beat rapidly as he watched and waited.

This is it, he thought to himself. I've found a water-snout, and once you find one, the others are sure to be nearby. Rutgers said so.

The mole was an excellent digger, almost as good as the badger. Soon he stopped, reached deep into the hole with his pointed nose, and began tugging on something. He backed up with great effort because he was dealing with something almost as large as he was. Twice it slipped from his tiny jaws, but at last he set it down next to the badger.

"Take a look at that," said the mole.

The badger said nothing for several moments. Then he sat down.

"How's that for strange?" said the mole, and he began pacing around, circling the object, checking it from all angles. "This will be one of the stranger things."

The badger still said nothing.

"You don't find one of these every day in the week," continued the mole. He was pacing faster now and had worked himself into a kind of frenzy. "Boy, oh boy," he muttered.

"That's a turnip," said the badger at last.

"What?" snapped the mole, stopping suddenly, his minute eyes shooting a piercing look at the badger. "Turnip, you say!"

"Turnip," said the badger. "Irregular maybe, but a turnip just the same."

"That's all you know," said the mole.

"Turnip," repeated the badger and slowly rose to his feet.

He was overcome with sadness and didn't know which way to turn. He only knew that he wanted to get away, away from this mole with his irregular turnip that should have been a water-snout. He needed time to think.

"Good-bye," said the badger almost inaudibly.

"Turnip indeed," said the mole. "The most important discovery in fifty years, and you say it's a turnip!"

The badger turned and lumbered slowly off into the woods.

Lost

18

Rutgers, Marshall, and Trippler were packing up, readying themselves to move on. They had waited for over four hours for the badger, and it was clear to them that he would not return. Each of them was silent as they gathered together, ready to continue their journey. Each of them was very sad and longed for the sight of the flat-headed badger without a name who had become their friend.

"Well," said Marshall absently, holding up his tattered map, "which way should we go?"

"I don't know," said Rutgers.

"I don't either," said Trippler.

Then Rutgers sat down.

"I can't do it," he said. "I just can't. I've got to know what happened to him."

"Me too," said Trippler.

"I know what you mean," said Marshall.

"Maybe he is tired of us," said Rutgers, "but I have to find out. What if he's in trouble and needs us? We've got to find him."

"You're right," said Trippler.

"Yes," said Marshall.

Suddenly they felt better, full of energy and purpose, and they set out to find their missing friend.

The badger was lost. He had wandered off to think—his mind in a haze—and had wandered into strange territory. His disappointment with the mole had dulled his senses and turned his eyes inward, and he had wandered for miles without taking any notice of where he was going. When he finally stopped and looked about him, he knew he was lost.

He was also hungry. It was dinnertime, and he hadn't eaten anything since the night before. He wondered why nothing looked familiar, but it was because he had wandered so far to the south. He was now far out of Resnick's Territory, in an area where he had never been before. He sat down— weak, hungry, and confused. A strong wind had come up, and it blew hard against him.

How did I get myself into this? he thought. Oh, how I miss my dear friends. If only I could see them, not to mention their food.

Just then an idea began to form in his mind. It disappeared at first, but soon it returned stronger than before, and he knew what to do. On the chance that his friends were looking for him, he would make them a trail; tracks to follow, tracks that they would know had been made by him.

He looked at the setting sun and judged that he had come far to the south. He would start in a northerly direction, and as he went he would dig holes. Every twenty yards he would dig a gigantic hole, and that would remind his friends of him and suggest to them that they were on his trail. He hadn't much strength, but he figured this was the only way.

And so he set out, stopping every twenty yards

to dig a gigantic
hole and pray that
his friends would find him.

Rutgers, Marshall, and Trippler had decided to limit their search to the land that lay to the south of the river. They figured that the badger would most likely not cross back to the other side of the river unless absolutely necessary. They had gone all the way to the ocean, searching every inch of ground, and they were now heading southeast. The wind was strong, and it was almost dusk. Marshall suggested stopping for dinner.

"Perhaps we should stop for dinner," said Marshall, peering westward at the setting sun.

"I don't think so," said Rutgers. "If we stop now, by the time we finish dinner it will be pitch dark, and we'll have to end our search for the night. I think we should press on."

Suddenly Trippler fell into a large hole.

"Help!" cried Trippler in a terrified mouse yelp as he fell to the bottom of the hole.

Rutgers and Marshall stopped and stared at the gigantic pit that opened before them.

"What's this?" said Marshall.

"Help, help!" cried Trippler from the bottom of the hole.

"I'll get you out," said Rutgers, and he jumped down into the hole to retrieve his friend.

Trippler took a firm grip on the cuff of Rutgers' sweat shirt with one paw—he was clutching his knapsack with the other—and held on tight as Rutgers climbed back up out of the hole. Then all three stood and stared at the hole.

"What a gigantic hole," said Marshall, peering with wonder at the sight that lay before him. The hole was at least three feet deep and easily six feet in diameter. "This is something unusual."

"That's the truth," said Trippler, checking his tiny body for bruises.

"I wonder what the purpose of this hole is," said Rutgers. "I don't think I've ever come across one like it. Little holes for homes and storage, yes, but nothing like this."

"I once came across one bigger," said Marshall, "but it was quite a different sort of hole. It was in the side of a mountain and looked as though it had been made by the rains. Rocks and earth had been washed away. But this was definitely made by someone for a purpose. Look how even it is. So carefully made."

"It's an amazing hole," said Rutgers.

"And not much fun to fall down," said Trippler. "Especially for a mouse."

They spent another few minutes puzzling over the hole, but they could come up with nothing and decided to move on.

"I guess that will just be one of those mysteries of life," said Rutgers in a tone that suggested a much older dog.

The night was pitch black, there was a strong cold wind, and the badger could go no further. He had continued to the north, having dug twelve holes, and he still had no idea in the world where he was. When he had finished the twelfth hole, he hadn't the strength to get up. There he lay at the bottom of the hole, unconscious from exhaustion.

A Familiar Face
19

Trippler fell into five more holes, and by then
Rutgers and Marshall were sure that the holes
were a sign of something.

"There's some meaning to these holes," said
Marshall as Rutgers brought Trippler up for the
sixth time.

All three animals sat down and thought.

"If you come upon something unusual—something you've never seen before—that's one thing,"

Marshall reasoned aloud. "It could just be that you haven't been around much and therefore haven't run across it before."

"True," said Trippler, wondering what Marshall was talking about.

"But," continued Marshall, "if the case is that you've been around a lot and one day or night you suddenly come across not one but a series—there's the key word—a series of things you never saw before, chances are there's more than chance involved."

"More than chance," muttered Trippler, who was completely lost.

"There lurks some reason here," said Marshall with a pompous tone creeping into his speech. "Now"—and he paused to emphasize his point—"what could it be?"

All three animals thought quietly to themselves.

"Who could dig such holes?" said Marshall. "And why?"

"The badger is the best digger I know," said Rutgers. "He could easily have dug them, but he's not here. He's missing."

"Aha!" said Marshall. "But maybe he was here! Maybe he's lost and figures we might be looking for him, and he dug these holes as a sign!"

"Of course!" said Rutgers and Trippler excitedly. "That's it!"

"Onward!" said Marshall, raising his map high.

"If you don't mind," said Trippler, "I'm going to bring up the rear. I'm glad these holes are a sign, but I'm tired of falling into them."

"I'll lead the way," said Rutgers. "To the badger!"

On they went, on into the black, cold, windy night. Now it was Rutgers who was falling into the holes. He fell into several. It was so dark that they had no hope of sighting the badger. Instead they kept calling out to him.

"Badger, badger," they called.

The wind was so strong that Trippler kept getting blown off the ground. So Marshall was now carrying Trippler under his arm. On they went, and it got colder and colder and windier and windier. Soon they could go no farther, and they crawled to the bottom of one of the holes for safety. Exhausted and discouraged, they slept.

The morning air was sharp and clear. Rutgers opened his eyes and looked directly into a familiar face—two eyes, closed now with sleep, set in a wide head. Two tiny ears stuck out on either side of the head, and a white stripe ran down the middle of the face.

"Badger, badger!" cried Rutgers, and the two eyes opened and looked at Rutgers.

Marshall and Trippler were awakened by the noise, and they stared in amazement.

"Badger!" they cried.

"Oh, my friends," said the badger, using the last of his strength to lift his head. "Oh, my friends, you found me!"

Marshall fed the badger all the bread and cheese he could eat, and soon the badger was strong enough to sit up and tell them what had happened.

"I went off after the mole," said the badger. "I was sure he had the snouts. I was positive, but I was wrong. All he has is a turnip!"

"You're back with us now," said Rutgers, "and that's the important thing. Together we can find the snouts."

The Discovery
of the Porcupines
20

Four and a half weeks had passed since the
search for the water-snouts had begun, and although Rutgers didn't talk about it, he had given
up. He followed along out of habit. Their wander-
ing had become a way of life, and Rutgers had
gotten used to it. He had grown thin from worry
and lack of food—he had lost his taste for it—and
his sweat shirt hung on him like a tent. His friends
all strongly doubted that the water-snouts would

ever be found, but they were so worried about Rutgers that they refused to give up. On they went, going through the motions of a search that they felt in their hearts was useless.

After finding the badger, they had crossed back across the river and had gone after the groundhog who had uncovered the unusual potato. Unfortunately, the groundhog was right, and that's exactly what it was. From there they had traveled to the north and had covered the entire North Woods.

It was Wednesday morning, and they were coming out of the woods, heading south. They could see the mountains on their left rising high into the clouds—a beautiful sight—but they were not in the mood for mountains.

Marshall took the lead as usual, holding part of his map in his right paw and part in his left. The map had fallen apart from so much use and travel, and it was almost impossible to read.

"It's turned cold again," said Trippler, grabbing the end of his muffler and holding it up to cover his frozen nose.

"It certainly has," said the badger.

"Maybe we should stop for brunch," said Marshall.

On the theory that they needed more energy,

Marshall had added two meals to their daily menu—brunch and tea.

"Rutgers could use some brunch, I'm sure," said Marshall.

"No, thank you," said Rutgers.

Rutgers knew that he would never again see his water-snouts, and nothing else mattered.

Trippler was the first to see the porcupines, and he gave a little start.

"Oh," cried Trippler, stopping so suddenly that he almost lost his balance.

Trippler had always felt that porcupines were strange looking, with their tiny heads and large bodies filled with long, pointed quills. Also, the porcupines were so far away that it was hard to make out exactly what they were.

"What is it?" said Marshall.

"Look there," said Trippler.

"Oh, my," said Marshall, and everyone stopped to look.

"What have we come across?" said the badger.

"Porcupines," said Marshall. "We're nearing their compound."

They moved forward, and soon they could all clearly make out the sight which lay before them. There were three porcupines, and they looked as if they were molting. Their coats were spotty, and one of them carried a small stick. All three were peering down at the ground and studying something.

"Hey, you porcupines," said Trippler, bounding up to say hello. "How are tricks?"

The porcupines turned to regard Trippler.

"Stop where you are," said the porcupine with the stick.

Trippler stopped.

"Who are you?" said the porcupine.

"Trippler," said Trippler, "a mouse," and he pointed behind him. "These are my friends."

"We're busy," said the porcupine.

"What have you got there?" said Trippler.

"Sick relatives," said the porcupine.

"That's too bad," said Trippler. "What happened?"

The porcupine explained that weeks ago he and his friends had found these relatives several miles from their compound. They had brought them back and tried steadily to revive them.

"No luck," said the porcupine, and the other

porcupines joined in. "Nothing works."

"Mind if I have a look?" said Trippler.

"Go ahead," said the porcupines.

Trippler moved forward and stared at the sick porcupines who lay lifeless on the ground.

"They don't look very lively, these relatives," said Trippler.

"We know," said the porcupine with the stick. "We've tried everything."

"Move up," said Trippler, calling to his friends. "Sick porcupines here."

Rutgers sat where he was, too upset to think of porcupines, but Marshall and the badger moved forward for a better look. They stared at the porcupines for several minutes, wondering if indeed they might not be dead. Not one of them appeared to be breathing. Not one of them moved an inch.

"Oh, dear," Marshall muttered to himself several times.

"Sick porcupines," said the badger.

Trippler kept calling out to Rutgers, urging him to take a look.

"Take a look at these," said Trippler, but Rutgers wouldn't move. He was too wrapped up in his own thoughts.

"I wish we could help," said Marshall to the porcupines. They were obviously expecting some kind of response and hovered about with pleading expressions. "There's not a doctor among us."

"Not even a nurse," said Trippler.

"I was a junior lifesaver in the badger brigade," said the badger, "but this is beyond me."

The porcupines said they understood and bid good-bye to their new acquaintances.

"So long," said the porcupines.

"Come on, Rutgers," said Marshall. "Let's go!" Rutgers slowly rose to his feet, picked up his knapsack, and started towards his friends. As he passed by the porcupines he glanced their way.

"Sorry about your relatives," said Rutgers.

"It can't be helped," said the porcupine with the stick.

"Good-bye," said Rutgers. Then he stopped dead in his tracks. He was already several feet from the porcupines, and he stood, stock-still, with his back to them. After a moment he turned very slowly around.

"Come on, Rutgers," said Trippler. "Let's go!" But Rutgers wouldn't budge.

"Time to move on," said Marshall.

"Oh, no," said Rutgers, very quietly and then again, "oh, no."

"What's wrong?" said Trippler.

"My snouts," said Rutgers. "Those are my snouts."

Reunion

21

Rutgers stood and cried. He cried long and hard—joy, relief, and exhaustion pouring out all at once.

"My snouts," he repeated through his sobs.

When at last his crying began to subside, Rutgers moved very slowly forward. He put his nose down and sniffed. He sniffed each snout, counting carefully.

"One, two, three, four, five, six, seven," he said.

"All safe." He looked up at his friends. "All safe," he repeated, smiling through his tears.

Then he turned back to his snouts and counted them several times. He turned each one over with his right front paw and checked the pricklers on the underneath side. Then he put his head down and moved forward, pushing at the snouts with his nose as if he were plowing or doing his spring planting. When he had had enough of that, he backed up and gave a sudden lunge, landing squarely on top of the snouts.

"Hello, you snouts," he said, and then he began rolling over and over, feeling the scratch of the pricklers and not minding a bit.

Marshall, Trippler, and the badger had already moved forward and were clustered around Rutgers.

"We've found the snouts! We've found the snouts," they cried.

As you can imagine, the porcupines were confused. They felt they deserved an explanation and demanded one in no uncertain terms.

"What's going on here?" said the porcupine with the stick, and the other porcupines joined in. "What's happening?"

As Rutgers rolled over and over amongst his snouts Marshall explained.

"What you have uncovered are not relatives but water-snouts," said Marshall, and he told them the whole story.

At first, the porcupines were dubious. They were convinced that they had found dear relatives and were not easily persuaded to change their minds. However, they did have to admit that Marshall's story might be valid. They had found their relatives on the beach exactly where the water-snouts were supposed to have been, and they had made their discovery a little over a month ago.

"Water-snouts?" said the porcupine with the stick. "Not relatives at all but water-snouts?"

"That's right," said Marshall.

At last the porcupines were convinced. They were certainly relieved to discover that they had no sick relatives after all, although one of the porcupines said he wouldn't mind finding some healthy relatives.

"There aren't so many of us porcupines around as there used to be," he said sadly.

Rutgers was still rolling over and over amongst his snouts and had now taken to barking and snapping at them.

"Oh, you wonderful snouts, you," he said between his barks, and then he bit them.

It was then that Resnick appeared.

"Here you are," he said, approaching from around a bend.

"Oh, Resnick," said Rutgers, looking up from his snouts. "We've found them! They're here! All safe!" And the other animals joined in.

"We've found the snouts! We've found the snouts!" they said all together.

"Glad to hear it," said Resnick, "but there's trouble. Bad trouble."

"What trouble could there be with snouts close at hand?" said Rutgers, turning back to his treasures. "All is well now."

"Not true," said Resnick.

"What's wrong?" said Marshall.

Resnick set down his mail pouch and took several deep breaths. It was obvious that he had been running for some distance.

"How did you find us?" said Trippler.

"Scouts," said Resnick, reaching into his mail pouch. "I have all points covered."

Resnick handed the message slip to Marshall, and everyone waited.

"What trouble can there be with snouts around?" Rutgers kept saying as Marshall studied the slip. "No trouble at all."

"You're wrong there," said Marshall when he had finished reading the message.

Then he told them.

The flood had reached Betty's dam. All the beavers for miles around had banded together to help save the area but had so far been unsuccessful. Betty's lodge would be destroyed in a matter of hours. She had worked straight through the night, gathering all the branches, twigs, and leaves within her grasp. But the job was too much for her, and the water continued to rise.

"That's terrible," said Trippler.

"Sure is," said Resnick.

Even the porcupines were concerned. They clustered closer together, their eyes bulging forward in their tiny heads.

"This isn't good," said Marshall, sitting back on his hind legs, ready to think things through. "We'll need an extensive meeting."

"No meetings," said Rutgers, and he stood up and began gathering his snouts. "To the rescue!"

"With all due respect," said Marshall, "we can't just go off on a rescue without a plan. We must formulate a plan."

"No meetings, no plans," said Rutgers as he dropped his water-snouts one by one into his knapsack. "We've got the snouts now. That's all we need."

"With all due respect," said Marshall, but Rutgers wouldn't let him finish.

"To the rescue!" said Rutgers.

"But what good are snouts?" said Trippler. "I don't see how snouts can help at a time like this."

"That's right," said Marshall. "With all due respect—"

"Never mind about that," said Rutgers, holding his knapsack firmly between his teeth. "I'm telling you we've got to go. Betty needs us!"

"He's right there," said Resnick.

"All right," said Marshall, "but with all due respect—"

"Let's go!" said Rutgers.

"I still don't see the good of snouts," said Trippler.

"You will!" said Rutgers. "Come on!"

The porcupines wanted to help too. Soon everyone was on his way, heading full speed ahead for Betty's dam.

Rescue

22

When they reached Betty's lodge, there was terrible confusion. The water had risen to a great height and was flowing fiercely. All kinds of animals were on either side of the water, carrying trees, sticks, branches, and leaves. Some of them even had pots, pans, and other possessions—anything that could be used to build a dam.

Several animals were in the water and had formed themselves into rows, passing things from one to another, piling and packing the dam with mud. But as soon as they got it rebuilt, the strong rush of water would wash it away, leaving them to start all over again from the beginning.

"Here we are!" shouted Rutgers as he led his friends to Betty's rescue. "We're here!"

Disregarding their fear of water, they jumped into the rising tide and swam toward their friend. Only Trippler stayed on dry land because he knew he would get washed downstream. He busied himself gathering leaves.

Rutgers still had his knapsack full of snouts gripped firmly between his teeth, and he swam as fast as he could to join Betty by the dam.

"I'm so glad you're here," said Betty as Rutgers approached. "But what are you doing with your knapsack in your mouth?"

"My snouts," said Rutgers. "They'll save the day!"

Rutgers turned his knapsack over and shook it hard, letting the water-snouts fall out and float on the surface of the water.

"Surround these snouts!" Rutgers announced in a loud voice to all the animals in the vicinity. "Don't let them get away!"

The animals were puzzled, but they were also desperate and ready to follow any instruction. They quickly formed themselves into a circle around the water-snouts, keeping them from being washed away in the strong rush of the flood.

Then Rutgers set to work. One by one he picked up the snouts and began shoring up the holes in the dam. The snouts were strong and just the right size, and their pricklers stuck into the branches, logs, and masses of twigs and mud and held them firmly. Even the strong rush of water couldn't budge them.

"Your snouts!" cried Betty. "They're saving the day!"

"Of course," said Rutgers as he wedged the last water-snout into the dam. "Get in there, you snout!"

The water continued to rise, but the dam was

high and the water-snouts held fast. The animals stood back and stared with wonder at the strong dam which held back the flood.

"It's working!" they all shouted together.

The word spread quickly.

"Water-snouts! That dog saved our dam with water-snouts!"

Soon all the animals knew what had happened.

"Hooray for Rutgers! Hooray for Rutgers and his water-snouts!"

Resnick had to get back to his Dispatch Office, and the porcupines had porcupine business to attend to, but Rutgers, Marshall, Trippler, and the badger stayed with Betty until the water was back down to its usual safe level. It was only a matter of three days. Then Rutgers took his water-snouts out from the dam, and Betty packed up the holes in her beaver way with mud and twigs, and things were back to normal.

Rutgers thanked his dear friends for helping him in the search, and before they headed off, each in the direction of his own home, they agreed to meet often.

They waved good-bye to Betty, and after crossing Rensler Brook they parted, going their separate ways. The badger headed north to his badger home, Marshall headed northwest to return to his very well-kept rabbit hole, and Trippler headed south pursuing the open road.

Rutgers took his water-snouts home with him— home to his square house with the flat roof that he had built for himself deep in the woods. He had decided not to bury them in the sand but to keep them with him, safe inside his house.

When he got to the house, he gave the door a strong push with his nose. The door swung open, and there was his warm, cozy room just as he had left it. He shut the door behind him and stood very still, holding his knapsack full of water-snouts firmly between his teeth. Then he turned the sack over and let the snouts fall to the floor.

"Hello, you wonderful snouts," he said. "Have a look around."

Format by Kohar Alexanian
Set in Linotype Times Roman
Composed and bound by
American Book–Stratford Press, Inc.
Printed by Halliday Lithograph Corp.
HARPER & ROW, PUBLISHERS, INCORPORATED